Groundwood Books / House of Anansi Press
110 Spadina Avenue, Suite 801, Toronto, Ontario M5V 2K4
or c/o Publishers Group West
1700 Fourth Street, Berkeley, CA 94710

We acknowledge for their financial support of our publishing
program the Canada Council for the Arts, the Government of
Canada through the Canada Book Fund (CBF) and the Ontario
Arts Council.

 Canada Council   Conseil des Arts    ONTARIO ARTS COUNCIL
for the Arts   du Canada   CONSEIL DES ARTS DE L'ONTARIO

Library and Archives Canada Cataloguing in Publication
Gay, Marie-Louise, author, illustrator
Any questions? / written and illustrated by Marie-Louise Gay.
ISBN 978-1-55498-382-7 (bound)
I. Title.
PS8563.A868A88 2014   jC813'.54   C2014-901337-X

The illustrations were done in watercolor, pencil, pastel, ink, colored
pencil and collage.
Design by Michael Solomon
Printed and bound in Malaysia

To all the children with
endless questions,
and to their parents, teachers
and librarians, who try to
answer them.

GROUNDWOOD BOOKS
HOUSE OF ANANSI PRESS
TORONTO   BERKELEY

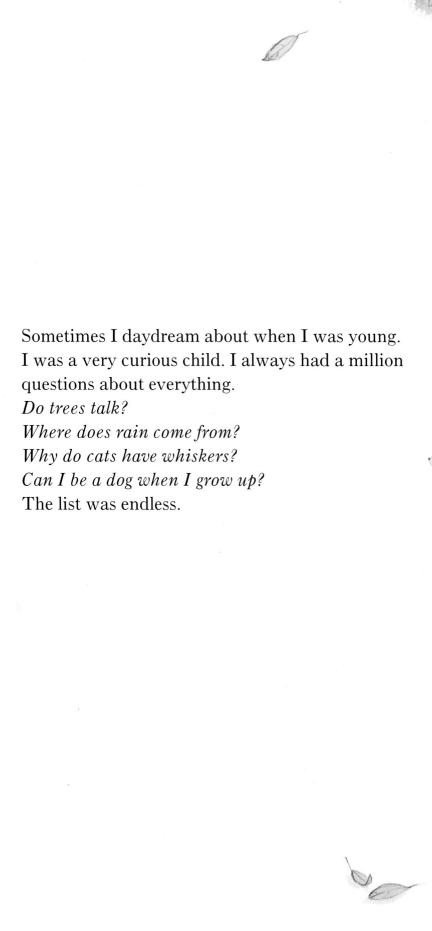

Sometimes I daydream about when I was young.
I was a very curious child. I always had a million
questions about everything.
Do trees talk?
Where does rain come from?
Why do cats have whiskers?
Can I be a dog when I grow up?
The list was endless.

When I meet children in schools or libraries,
I see that nothing has changed. Children are
as curious as ever.
They ask me questions all the time…
lots and lots of questions!
And why not? If you don't ask questions,
how on earth will you get any answers?

Hmmm, let's see … I don't have a hamster
or a rabbit,
but I do have a goldfish.
My favorite color is purple.
And sadly, my cat can't fly.
Where does a story start?
Now that's a good question.
A story always starts on a blank
white page, like this … ⟶
If you stare long enough at
a blank piece of paper,
anything can happen …

For example, a blank white page could become a ... snowstorm.

But what if my story started on old yellowish paper?
Would it be different?

What if my paper was sea blue?

Or maybe a stormy purplish gray?

Or jungly green?

IT COULD BE A HORROR STORY. HAR HAR HAR!

DOES EVERY STORY START WITH A DIFFERENT COLOR?

Or even midnight black!

Not always. Sometimes a story starts with
words or ideas floating out of nowhere.
Some words are captured and written down …

while others get thrown out
or carefully put away in a drawer for future use.
Until slowly, slowly, a story emerges…

Then suddenly, little scribbles and doodles
appear here and there,
between and around the words.
Spots of color splash silently
on the page and become shapes,
characters and ideas.

"Once upon a time, a million years ago, or was it only yesterday, in a dark, green, mossy forest, where the sun rarely shone and where the trees were so old that they could hardly walk, let alone dance, there lived a ...
there lived a... a... a...

THERE LIVED A...?

THERE LIVED A...?

THERE LIVED A...?

Believe it or not, there are times when I don't have any
ideas at all. My mind is a blank.

Or worse, I might get an idea that doesn't fit into
the story. Like this one...

So I have to use my imagination. Try out new ideas.
Let's see … what about …

A big bad wolf?

And three little pigs?

A singing rabbit?

A ferocious snail?

A lost princess?

A powerful wizard?

But sometimes that doesn't work either.
So I go back to my drawing table. I start to sketch stars
and spirals, snails, rabbits or a few tiny caterpillars …

I draw and paint. I cut and paste.
I let my mind wander ...

I shake my ideas around and turn them upside down
and look at them flying out the window like a flock of
birds. Suddenly, I *know* who lives in the forest … a giant,
a shy young giant with birds nesting in his hair.
His story starts here …

THE SHY YOUNG GIANT

Once upon a time, a million years ago, or was it only yesterday, in a dark, green, mossy forest, where the sun rarely shone and where the trees were so old that they could hardly walk, let alone dance, there lived a young giant. He was the guardian of the forest. It was his job to protect it. His father had done this, as well as his grandmother before him.

The young giant watered the forest when the trees were thirsty and stamped out any fire caused by lightning or fireflies.
He planted mushrooms and flowers between the toes of the trees, which made them laugh. Trees are very ticklish, as you know.

The giant read stories to the trees to help them grow. Some trees liked poems, while others loved adventure stories. Of course, the skinny birch trees preferred love stories. So he was a very busy young giant.
He was also a very shy young giant. He was so shy that he couldn't chase away the birds that nested in his hair. He was so shy that he would hide if he heard someone coming near. Not an easy thing to do if you are a giant...

One cold, gray autumn day, when the trees had just started losing their leaves, revealing their well-kept secrets — hidden birds' nests, lost kites and the dreams of those who had slept in their cool, leafy summer shadows — the giant heard something. Thundering footsteps on the ground. Leaves rustling. Snatches of song. Branches snapping.

A grrrrowling sound! Someone or something was coming his way. The shy young giant hid behind a huge rock. He stopped breathing. He did not move an inch or even blink an eyelash. He desperately hoped that whoever or whatever was coming towards him wouldn't see him. The noises grew louder and louder. All of a sudden...

GROWL!

STOMP!

All of a sudden … all of a sudden … It's your turn!
What do *you* think happens next?

GR-R-R-R!

SNAP!

All of a sudden...
It burst out of the bushes!
It was a huge horrible, ~~gigantic~~
~~ugly~~, hairy, prickly ~~beest~~
beast! It was purple! It had
shark's tee~~e~~th, ~~bare~~ bear
claws and a long, spiny, slimy
green tail. The beast was
~~ferochus~~
~~ferosh~~ scary
and verrry
hungry!
Or verry
mad!
Or both!

UH-OH!

So, the abominable,
wretched, ferocious beast
ran through the forest
gnashing his teeth,
biting trees and bushes,
devouring mushrooms and
berries, flowers and
rotten apples.
The beast chased birds
and butterflies,
rabbits and foxes,
and wolfed down
all the leftover dreams...

The dreadful, ghastly, disgusting purple beast swallowed up the river, the frogs and the fish. He squished the snails and the caterpillars. The beast would have gobbled up the stars, the moon and the planets, but he was too fat to jump up and reach them.

The beast snarled and growled! The beast shrieked and howled!!

Your ideas are brilliant and your beast is magnificent... I mean, your beast is absolutely horrible! Do you want to see what happens when the giant meets the beast?

YES!

GR-R-R-R-R

The beast caused such an uproar and confusion that the giant couldn't stay hidden anymore. He couldn't be shy anymore.
He had to do something.
First, he whispered, "Stop!"
Then he shouted, "Stop!"

Then he roared, "S-S-STOP!!!"
The horrible purple beast stopped dead in his tracks.
He stared up at the giant.
The giant blushed. He had never roared before.

"Who are you?" asked the giant.
"I'm a beast," whispered the beast. "A horrible, dreadful beast."
"Do you have a name?" asked the giant.
The beast's cheeks turned crimson.
"Fluffy," mumbled the beast.
"Well, Fluffy, why are you gobbling up my forest? Are you hungry?"

WHO ARE YOU?

I'M A BEAST.

"No," muttered the beast. "I was lonely and angry and ... sad."
"It's hard to make friends when you are a ferocious beast,"
said the giant. "Would you like me to read you a story?"
The beast's eyes widened. His heart was beating very fast.
"Yes," he whispered. No one had ever read a story
to him in his whole beastly life.

The shy young giant pulled a book out of his pocket and started reading in his soft, rumbly voice. The trees crowded silently around the beast and the giant. The children came out from behind the trees as did the birds,

the rabbits, the snails and other forest creatures.
"Once upon a time," read the giant, "a million
years ago, or was it only yesterday, in a dark, green, mossy
forest, where the sun rarely shone and where the trees..."

The story echoed throughout the forest. Words of all shapes
and sizes, figments of the imagination and brilliant ideas
threaded their way through the tree branches and
floated up into the sky.

Owls hooted softly. The trees rustled. The beast sighed. They all listened with their ears and their hearts wide open. The moon rose as the giant finally whispered, "The End."

THE END ~~BEGINNING~~

Where do your ideas come from?
Some ideas come from my imagination or my daydreams. Others are inspired by my childhood memories. Some ideas creep up on me when I least expect it—when I travel or meet children in schools or just happen to look out the window.

How many books do you make in one day?
It takes me at least a year to write and illustrate a book, sometimes longer. In a day, I am lucky if I write one good paragraph.

Do you put a cat in every book?
I have probably drawn at least 3,409 cats in my life, so there must be one in almost every book. I think you will have to check.

How did you learn to draw?
I started doodling in the margins of my school books when I was sixteen or so. My doodles became drawings when I attended art school, where I learned to paint and draw hands and faces, cars and clouds, shadows and sunlight, elephants and snails … Since then I have been drawing every day. The more you draw, while keenly observing the world around you, the more you learn.

How many books have you written?
I have written and/or illustrated about seventy books.

Which is your favorite book?
That is like asking a mother who is her favorite child … Stella or Sam? Caramba? Roslyn Rutabaga? Charlie or his little brother, Max? I just can't choose one. Can you?

Do you draw with a pencil?
I draw my outlines with a pencil or a pen. Then I paint with watercolors or inks, acrylics or gouache. I also use pastels and colored pencils. In some books I add collage, created with handmade Japanese paper, torn bits of newspaper or scraps of sheet music.

Can you draw a horse?
No, even after all these years of drawing, my horses look like big dogs with crooked legs. Are *you* good at drawing horses?

YOU MADE IT! HERE ARE THE ANSWERS TO YOUR QUESTIONS.

Are you Stella?
Stella is a character I created from a few of my childhood memories as well as memories of my two boys when they were little, with a bit of imagination, a dash of humor and voilà! Stella was born. Then along came Sam…

Can your cat fly?
Unfortunately not. But that doesn't keep him from trying.

Have you ever touched a snake?
Yes, just like Stella in *Stella, Fairy of the Forest*, when I was little I would pick up garter snakes and pet them. My friends were impressed.

Can you write a story about me?
Maybe I will. Roslyn Rutabaga was inspired by a very inventive and creative little girl in my neighborhood. So watch out! You might become a rabbit in one of my stories.

Do you write all day, from morning to night? Or do you have time to read or do other things?
I write every day, but I always find time to read. I think all writers are great readers. I also ride my bicycle, play tennis or lie on my back on the grass and look at clouds.

What is your favorite color?
Purple. But some days green is my favorite color. Or orange. It depends on the weather.

Where does a story start?
A story often starts on a blank white page. When the first tiny glimmer of an idea appears, it inspires words, images and colors, which fuel the imagination. Slowly a story emerges with all its possibilities and choices. Then it is up to the author to explore the best way to tell the story.

What inspired you to write this book?
All your questions!